JULIO'S MAGIC

ARTHUR DORROS ❧ **COLLAGES BY ANN GRIFALCONI**

▰HARPERCOLLINS*PUBLISHERS*

Julio's Magic

Text copyright © 2005 by Arthur Dorros

Collages copyright © 2005 by Ann Grifalconi

Manufactured in China by South China Printing Company Ltd.

Library of Congress Cataloging-in-Publication Data is available on request.

ISBN 0-06-029004-8 — ISBN 0-06-029005-6 (lib. bdg.)

Typography by Matt Adamec

1 2 3 4 5 6 7 8 9 10

❖

First Edition

For Bob, Michiyo, Luis, Felicidad, and all the artists
—A.D.

To all the wonderful Oaxacan craftsmen and their families
whom I have gotten to know and admire over the years!
—A.G.

Julio woke up before the light. He heard dogs barking, heard burro loudly braying, heard rooster calling for the day. In between all these sounds, he heard a quiet rustling, a whisper from the trees.

Julio leaped out of bed. Today he was going to the mountain with Iluminado, to find wood.

"With that wood I could win the contest!" thought Julio.

The contest was in the city far away, for the best wood carvings in all the land. The prize was more money than most villagers, who were farmers, could make in half a year.

Julio had learned about wood carving from Iluminado. All the other carvers said Iluminado was the best carver in the village. But Iluminado never entered the contest.

"My contest is with myself," he said, "to make the best carvings I can."

Julio did want to enter the contest.

He started to run out of his house.

"Julio!" his mother called. He had to help harvest corn. With water from the river, Julio's family would have good crops this year.

Julio helped his father pile the corn high in a cart.

"¡Listo!" said Julio's father, telling him he was ready and Julio could now go.

"Where are you running to?" asked Fredi, who lived next door.

"I'm going to find wood that talks to me," said Julio.

"You think wood can talk?" Fredi shouted back.

"Maybe it will sing," said Julio.

Fredi did not understand. His was not a family of wood-carvers. Neither was Julio's family.

Iluminado had told Julio, "Wood can talk to you. It will tell you what it wants to be."

Julio raced toward Iluminado's house in the hills. He followed the trail past houses just awakening, past the smell of warm tortilla breakfasts baking, past goats and pigs and cows stomping in the fields, past a parade of wooden dancers that Angel's family was painting.

Angel had won the carving contest last year. "Lucky for me Iluminado does not enter the contest. Maybe I can win again this year," said Angel.

Julio hurried on, past the Santiago family's house. The Santiago family was famous for its animals. Quirino's name came from the sound, *qui, quiri, qui,* of roosters like those he carved.

Maestro was one of the first people in the village to become a carver, and he was still one of the finest. Julio took the path by Octavio's house full of angels. "I don't think anyone can carve better angels than Octavio, or better animals than the Santiagos," thought Julio.

As Julio arrived, Iluminado sat carving.

When Julio was a little boy, he had first passed Iluminado's house on his way to gather firewood with his father. Julio had wanted to watch and watch as animals and people leaped to life from the wood.

Later, Iluminado showed Julio how to paint the wooden figures, and when Julio got older, he showed him how to carve, too.

Now Iluminado touched the wood, finding his way with his fingers as he carved. His eyesight was going dark, and he could not see as he used to.

"Hola," said Julio.

"Finally, you are here," Iluminado joked. "My burro,
Alegría, is hungry. She has tried to eat everything in sight."

Julio looked at Iluminado's brown fields. He did not see much for Alegría to eat,
nor for Iluminado. It had been a year without much rain, and up here, where there
was no river water, the crops had not grown well.

"¡*Vámonos*, Alegría!" Iluminado said, as they started the long climb to the mountainside where the best wood for carving grew. Julio saw his school below, with its huge satellite dish on top for receiving lessons that he saw there on television.

"Lessons from outer space," Iluminado joked.

"The school does look like something from outer space," thought Julio. But he knew the television lessons came from the big city where the carving contest would be.

"You should enter the contest," Julio said.

"I do not think so," Iluminado answered.

When they reached the
forest, they sat in the shade of an
old copal tree.

They watched ants scurrying and
grasshoppers leaping, heard the whir of wings
as hummingbirds darted at cactus flowers.

"Ideas for carvings all around," said Iluminado. He
touched the curving branch of a copal tree. "This will make
a good dragon."

Julio found a piece of
wood that with its shape
whispered "burro," and
another, "lizard." But he
needed something different.
He climbed into the tree.
Branches twisted this way and that.
A jungle of shapes danced around him.
Then he knew what he would carve.
He asked Iluminado for the saw and carefully
cut some branches.

Back at home, Julio carved every chance he got.

Little by little, a jungle filled with animals took shape.

Julio carved animals that hung from tree branches and swung from vines.

"Those are the best carvings you have ever done," said Julio's mother as he placed them in a box and slid them under his bed.

Julio went to visit Iluminado and helped him harvest heavy winter squash.

He looked at the small pile of squash and the little bit of corn that would not feed Iluminado for the winter. Iluminado looked thinner, too.

The carvers in the village sold their carvings, which helped, especially when the crops were not good.

Iluminado had sold some carvings recently, but not many.

He carved slowly now, yet he still carved well.

"You should enter the contest," Julio urged again.

Iluminado thought for a moment. "Maybe," he said.

Julio continued to work on his carvings.

"¡Fantástico!" said Angel when he saw them.

Even Fredi told Julio, "Maybe you could win the contest."

Angel had packed his carvings and was taking them to mail to the far-off contest.

Carver after carver sent carvings. It was only a week until the contest began.

The next day Julio hurried to see Iluminado.

"Here," said Iluminado, showing Julio a group of twirling musicians.

Julio could hear the music.

"How will I paint them?" Iluminado asked. He was still one of the best carvers, but because his eyesight was failing, it was difficult to paint.

"I will help," Julio said.

Each day he painted as he had learned with Iluminado, using wild stripes and spots, shapes and colors of all kinds.

"Nature is so amazing," Iluminado said, "what people can do is try to make different beauties."

They packed and sent the carvings.

The carvers waited. Every day they asked one another, "Have you heard from the contest? Did you get a letter?"

Because of the carvings he had done, they especially asked Julio.

"Did you get a letter yet?" Fredi kept asking.

One afternoon, a letter came to the village. It was addressed to Iluminado.

"Read it to me," Iluminado asked Julio.

It began, "We are pleased to inform you . . ."

Iluminado had won the contest.

Julio smiled.

Iluminado smiled too. "Thank you," he said. "Maybe next year you will win!"

At home, Julio took the box he had packed from under the bed. He fitted the pieces of his jungle together. "Next year," he said.